D0859468

Once Upon a CHRISTMAS EVE

BY KATHY-JO WARGIN
ILLUSTRATIONS BY BRUCE LANGTON

All inquiries should be addressed to:

Mitten Press

An imprint of Ann Arbor Media Group LLC

2500 S. State Street

Ann Arbor, MI 48104

877.722.2264

Printed and bound in Canada.

09 08 07 06 05 1 2 3 4 5

Library of Congress Cataloging-in-Publication Data

Wargin, Kathy-jo.

Once upon a Christmas Eve / by Kathy-jo Wargin ; illustrated by Bruce Langton.

p. cm.

Summary: On Christmas Eve, Kate leaves the warm farmhouse and heads into the snowy forest, hoping to hear the animals speak on this special night.

ISBN-13: 978-1-58726-290-6 (hardcover : alk. paper)

ISBN-10: 1-58726-290-8 (hardcover)

[1. Christmas--Fiction. 2. Animals--Fiction.] I. Langton, Bruce, ill. II. Title.

PZ7.W234Leg 2005

[E]--dc22

2005008265

Book and jacket design by Somberg Design

www.sombergdesign.com

It was almost midnight on Christmas Eve, the moment when legend says all animals are given the gift of speech. Kate was snug in her bed, wondering if the legend was true.

Unable to sleep, she dressed in winter clothes and slipped out of the house unnoticed. The sweeping drifts of snow slowed her as she made her way from the farmhouse to the distant edge of the forest. The soft light from her lantern set the snow aglow while her boots made a path through the trees.

Kate wanted to hear animals speak and was wondering what they would say. Deciding to stay until she heard them, she nestled into the branches of an old pine tree and waited.

Kate sat very still and listened. She heard the gentle scrape of pine trees rubbing in the wind and the quiet sounds of birds huddling to stay warm. She heard the soft winter footsteps of mice upon the snow and the once-in-awhile crack of icy branches in the night. The wind began to blow a bit harder and she pulled her scarf a bit tighter. She waited and listened, but didn't hear any animals speak.

She felt cold from the wind and sad in her heart. Deciding to go home, she looked back upon her path.

But her footsteps had disappeared.

All she saw were mounds of newly fallen snow between the evergreens and birch. Then, as she looked closer to find where her path might have been, her lantern sputtered and spat and with a wisp of smoke went dark.

Tears began to well up in her eyes as she looked through the darkness all around her. She tried to walk carefully through the trees, but found herself deeper in the woods. Everything seemed strange and unfamiliar, and soon Kate realized she was lost. In the darkest part of the woods with no one near to hear her, Kate cupped her face into her mittens and began to cry, certain she would be lost forever.

As her sad cries echoed through the forest, one small bird landed upon her shoulder and the brightest of stars rose above her.

"It is time,"
said the owl
as it swooped overhead,
"it is time that we journey
to the new baby's bed."

"I will lead,"
said the deer
as she bowed on her knees.
"I will lead us to the manger
that waits in the trees."

Kate heard the animals speak! It wasn't long before the owl and deer began to make their way through the forest, with other animals joining them. Raccoons scrambled down from snowy perches and beavers came out from their round winter homes. Foxes and hares walked slowly in pairs, while families of moose gathered in behind them.

And from further away,
the cows ambled from
snow-laden hills, and oxen
strayed from valleys far
beyond. Horses came in
from faraway stables, and as she
watched them make their way, Kate
wanted nothing more than to go with
them. So she slipped in, and the
animals welcomed her.

"We will sing,"
said the birds,
as they flew from the birch,
"to announce he's arrived
in our own woodland church."

"And we'll hum,"
said the queen
of the now waking bees,
"the most beautiful sounds
of our sweet symphonies."

"I will guide,"
said the wolf,
"the lost lambs and sheep,
and lead them to the baby
that lays fast asleep."

"We shall bring,"
said the geese
as they took to the air,
"brilliant gifts on our wings
to the babe that sleeps there."

Kate walked with the animals all the way to the tallest pine in the forest. Beneath it was a small manger made from sticks and branches. The animals hushed as they gathered around it. As the light of one brilliant star shined upon them all, a great mother bear came out of her den, holding a doll made of straw.

"This is," said the bear,
"the best night of all,
for a babe long ago
was born in a stall.

"And we gather," she said,
"beneath this star's light,
to speak to each other on
each Christmas night."

Then, as if laying her own child to sleep, the mother bear laid the straw doll softly upon a bed of hay, and beneath the broad and beaming light of the Christmas Star whispered, "Noel." And softly, all of the other animals whispered "Noel" in return.

The next morning, Kate woke in her bed. Her quilt was neatly tucked around her and her pillow felt warm. Like a distant memory, she remembered the animals, the beautiful forest, and the simple doll made of straw.

But as Kate looked around her room, she thought it must have been a dream, for her coat was hanging right where it had been the day before, and her scarf and mittens were dry. In an instant, her heart felt heavy and sad. Kate believed the legend must not be true.

But when Kate climbed out of her blankets, she noticed a small bundle lying at the foot of her bed. And there it lay, the simple baby doll made of straw. Kate held it in her arms and smiled.

And that Christmas morning, while the world sang of joy, Kate held the doll close to her heart and looked out her window to say, "Noel to you, my dear friends. Noel to all of you too."

Merry Christmas